TIGERS FOR DINNER

Ruskin Bond has been writing for over sixty years, and now has over 120 titles in print—novels, collections of stories, poetry, essays, anthologies, and books for children. His first novel, *The Room on the Roof*, received the prestigious John Llewellyn Rhys Prize in 1957. He has also received the Padma Shri, and two awards from the Sahitya Akademi—one for his short stories and another for his writings for children. In 2012, the Delhi government gave him its Lifetime Achievement Award.

Born in 1934, Ruskin Bond grew up in Jamnagar, Shimla, New Delhi and Dehradun. Apart from three years in the UK, he has spent all his life in India, and now lives in Mussoorie with his adopted family.

A shy person, Ruskin says he likes being a writer because, 'When I'm writing there's nobody *watching* me. Today, it's hard to find a profession where you're not being watched!'

Sunaina Coelho works in Mumbai as a freelance designer, creating animation for television and the Internet and illustrating for books and magazines. She studied animation film design at the National Institute of Design, Ahmedabad. She likes to draw, read, cook (and eat!), play with her cat, and whenever possible, travel and see new places.

TIGERS FOR DINNER

TALL TALES
BY JIM CORBETT'S KHANSAMA

RUSKIN BOND

Illustrated by SUNAINA COELHO

RED
TURTLE

Published in
RED TURTLE by Rupa Publications India Pvt. Ltd. 2013
7/16, Ansari Road, Daryaganj
New Delhi 110002

Sales Centres:

Allahabad Bengaluru Chennai
Hyderabad Jaipur Kathmandu
Kolkata Mumbai

ISBN: 978-81-291-2114-1

10 9 8 7 6 5 4 3 2 1

The moral right of the author has been asserted.

Typeset in Myriad Pro 16/30

Printed by Thomson Press India Ltd., Faridabad

For my grandchildren, the adventurous five—
Siddharth, Shrishti, Gautam, Atish and Vaishnavi.
Have fun, stay happy!

* CONTENTS *

INTRODUCTION

Did Mehmoud really exist, and did he really have these adventures? These are questions I am often asked.

When I was a small boy we did have a cook called Mehmoud, and among his testimonials was one from the great Jim Corbett, praising Mehmoud's culinary skills. We had no reason to doubt it was not genuine.

As to the tales themselves, well—like all good storytellers, Mehmoud was given to a little exaggeration, so we must allow him some poetic licence. As his loyal fan, I swallowed everything he told me.

One of his specialities was Turtle Soup; but out of respect for Red Turtle, the publisher of this book, I am suppressing the recipe.

Ruskin Bond

.1.

JUNGLE COOK

y favourite stories as a child?

Well, it would be hard to beat the tales—short or tall—that I heard from Mehmoud, who was our *khansama*, or cook, when I was five or six years old.

My parents didn't tell me many stories. Mum was busy with her parties, and Dad with his stamp collection; that is, when he wasn't in his office. I had the house and the grounds to myself, but there was

no one to talk to, expect the flowers. The cosmos were good listeners. They nodded politely when I spoke to them. The roses looked away; they were very snobbish. The marigolds were friendly enough, provided I didn't pick them.

So I would wander into the kitchen, to see what Mehmoud was making for lunch. And to taste the kofta curry or the pulao rice, just to make sure the taste was right. Since then, I've been a curry taster all my life.

Mehmoud was a good cook and in many ways, my best friend (there being no children on the premises); but he was also a great storyteller.

You see, before coming to us he'd worked for Jim Corbett, the great *shikari*, who'd shot a great number of man-eating tigers, apart from other dangerous denizens of the jungle.

'Did you see him shoot a tiger?' I asked.

'Oh, many times,' said Mehmoud. 'A tiger a week— that was nothing to Carpet-sahib!'

'Did the tigers come to the house, or did you go looking for them?'

'Carpet-sahib went after them. Most of the time we were in the camps, and I had to do my cooking in the open. Not an easy job, being a jungle cook. Usually the salt was missing, and everyone would complain.'

'My mother says you put too much salt in the food.'

'That's so I don't forget it. Better a salty dish than

a tasteless one. Don't you agree, baba?'

'And too many chillies,' I added.

'A chilli a day keeps the doctor away. That's

what my grandfather used to say, and he was an Unani—a doctor of natural medicine from the old Persian system. A little masala, a little turmeric—and you won't need a medic! My grandfather was a wise man, he taught me to read and write in Urdu, but I never went to school—had to earn a living from a very young age. So I learnt to cook—it's not a bad way of making a living.'

'You're not a bad cook.'

'So tell your parents to increase my salary.'

'Then be careful with the salt.'

'You're a salty boy. And saucy. Try one of these koftas. I knew you'd come, so I made an extra kofta.'

'Thank you, Mehmoud. But tell me about Corbett. And tigers. Did you see a tiger?'

'Of course I did. There were tigers all over the

place. Bang, bang, bang! Carpet-sahib kept firing, and the tigers kept falling. Man-eaters, cattle-eaters, child-eaters. One of them took my *masalchi* when we were in camp. Took him from the tent we were sharing. Dragged him out by his feet and carried him away while he screamed. That tiger was too fast for Carpet-sahib. By the time the camp aroused, both tiger and *masalchi* had vanished. We found his bones in the morning.'

'What's a *masalchi*?' I asked.

'The boy who helped me. He helped me prepare the meat and vegetables, and washed all the dishes afterwards. He was a big loss. For two weeks I had to manage everything on my own. We couldn't get another *masalchi*. No applications. And I had to sleep alone for the rest of the time we were in camp.

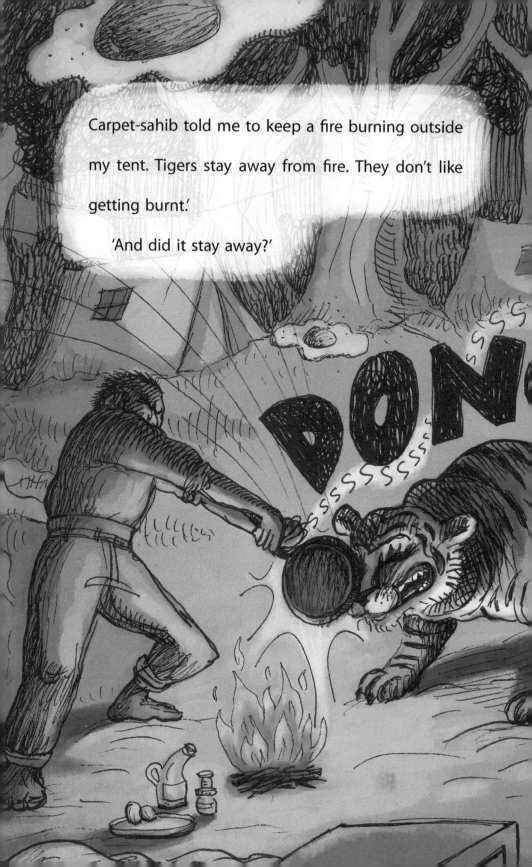

'No, the brute came again. Stuck its head in at the tent opening, looking for another juicy *masalchi*. But I was ready for it. I had just been frying some eggs, and my frying pan was as hot as hell-fire, and with it I struck the tiger on its nose!'

'You're a brave man, Mehmoud. What did the tiger do?'

'It didn't like it. You see, tigers have very sensitive noses. That's why they have such a strong sense of smell. Their noses lead them to their prey. But a burnt nose can be very painful, especially for a tiger. And I'd singed its whiskers too. Tigers don't like losing their whiskers, just like army generals!'

'So what happened?'

'It let out a roar, leapt into the air, fell backwards into the fire, let out another roar, and fled into the jungle. For an hour or more we could hear it roaring with agony.'

'You were very brave, Mehmoud. What did everyone say when you told them what you had done?'

'They didn't believe me, baba. They said I was making it all up; that the tiger had taken off after burning its paw in the fire. I showed Carpet-sahib the tiger's whiskers stuck to the bottom of my frying pan, but he only laughed and said I could serve tiger soup for dinner.'

'But you were a hero, Mehmoud!'

'Yes, baba, I'm glad you think so. Have another kofta.'

.2.
EXCITING ENCOUNTERS

The following day, Mehmoud was making lamb chops. I liked lamb chops. Mehmoud knew I liked them, and he had an extra chop ready for me, just in case I felt like a pre-lunch snack.

'What was Jim Corbett's favourite dish?' I asked, while dealing with the succulent chop.

'Oh, he liked roast duck. Used to shoot them as they flew up from the *jheel.*'

'What's a *jheel*, Mehmoud?'

'A shallow sort of lake. In places you could walk about in the water. Different types of birds would come there in the winter—ducks and geese and all kinds of *baglas*—herons, you call them. The *baglas* are not good to eat, but the ducks make a fine roast.

'So we camped beside the *jheel* and lived on roast duck for a week until everyone was sick of it.'

'Did you go swimming in the *jheel*?'

'No, it was full of *muggers*—those long-nosed crocodiles—they'll snap you up if you come within their range! Nasty creatures, those *muggermuch*. One of them nearly got me.'

'How did that happen, Mehmoud-bhai?'

'Oh, baba, just the memory of it makes me shudder! I'd given everyone their dinner and retired to my tent. It was a hot night and we couldn't sleep. Swarms of mosquitoes rose from the *jheel*, invaded the tent, and attacked me on the face and arms and feet. I dragged my camp cot outside the tent, hoping the breeze would keep the mosquitoes away. After some time they moved on, and I fell asleep, wrapped up in my bedsheet. Towards dawn, I felt my cot quivering, shaking. Was it an earthquake? But no one else was awake. And then the cot started moving! I sat up, looked about me. The cot was moving steadily forward in the direction of the water. And beneath it, holding us up, was a beastly crocodile!

'It gave me the fright of my life, baba. A *muggermuch* beneath my bed, and I upon it! I cried out for help. Carpet-sahib woke up, rushed out of his tent, his gun in his hands. But it was still dark, and all he could see was my bed moving rapidly towards the *jheel*.

'Just before we struck the water, I leapt from the cot, and ran up the bank, calling for help. Carpet-sahib saw me then. He ran down the slope, firing at the moving cot. I don't know if he hit the horrible creature, but there was a big splash, and it disappeared into the *jheel*.'

'And did you recover the cot?'

'No, it floated away and then sank. We did not go after it.'

'And what did Corbett say afterwards?'

'He said I had shown great presence of mind. He said

he'd never seen anyone make such a leap for safety!'

'You were a hero, Mehmoud!'

'Thank you, baba. There's time for another lamb chop, if you're hungry.'

'I'm hungry,' I said. 'There's still an hour left to lunchtime. But tell me more about your time with Jim Corbett. Did he like your cooking?'

'Oh, *he* liked it well enough, but his sister was very fussy.'

'He had his sister with him?'

'That's right. He never married, so his sister looked after the household and the shopping and everything connected to the kitchen—except when we were in camp. Then I had a free hand. Carpet-sahib wasn't too fussy about his food, especially when he was out hunting. A sandwich or paratha would keep him going. But if he had guests, he felt he had to give them the best, and then it was hard work for me.

'For instance, there was the Raja of Janakpur, a big, fat man who was very fond of eating—between meals, during meals and after meals. I don't know why he

bothered to come on these *shikar* trips when he could have stayed at home in his palace and feasted day and night. But he needed trophies to hang on the walls of his palace. You were not considered a great king unless your walls were decorated with the stuffed heads of tigers, lions, antelopes, bears— anything that looked dangerous. The Raja could eat and drink all day, but he couldn't go home without a trophy. So he would be hoisted on to an elephant, and sit there in state, firing away at anything that moved in the jungle. He seldom shot anything, but Carpet-sahib would help him out by bringing down a stag or a leopard, and congratulating the Raja on his skill and accuracy.

'They weren't all like that, but some of the rajas were stupid or even mad. And the Angrej-sahibs—

the English—were no better. They too had to prove their manliness by shooting a tiger or a leopard. Carpet-sahib was always in demand, because he lived at the edge of the jungle and knew where to look for different animals.

'The Raja of Janakpur was safe on an elephant, but one day he made the mistake of walking into the jungle on foot. He hadn't gone far when he met a wild boar running at him. A wild boar may not look very dangerous, but it has deadly tusks and is quick to use them. Before the Raja could raise the gun to his shoulder, the pig charged at him. The Raja dropped his gun, turned and ran for his life. But he couldn't run very fast or very far. He tripped and fell, and the boar was almost upon him when I happened along, looking for twigs to make a fire. Luckily, I had a small axe in my hand. I struck the boar over the head. It turned and rammed one of its tusks into my thigh. I struck at it again and again, till it fell dead at my feet. The Raja was nowhere in sight.

'As soon as he got into camp, he sent for his servants and made a hurried departure. Didn't even thank me for saving his life!'

'Were you hurt badly, Mehmoud?'

'I was out of action for a few days. The wound took time to heal. My new *masalchi* did all the cooking, and the food was so bad that most of the guests left in a hurry. I still have the scar. See, baba!'

Mehmoud drew up his pyjamas and showed me a deep scar on his right thigh.

'You were a hero, Mehmoud,' I said. 'You deserved a reward!'

'My reward is here, baba, preparing these lamb chops for you. Come on, have another. Your parents won't notice if they run short at lunch!'

.3.

'GOOD SHOT, MEHMOUD!'

t was a long, hot summer that year, but a summer in the plains has its compensations—such as mangoes and melons and lychees and custard apples. The fruit-seller came to our house every day, a basket of fresh fruit balanced on his head. One morning, I entered the kitchen to find a bucket full of mangoes, and Mehmoud busy making a large jug of mango milkshake.

'Pass me some ice, baba, you'll find it in the

bucket. You can have a milkshake now, and another with your lunch. Carpet-sahib thought highly of my milkshakes. During the mango season, he'd have two glasses of mango milkshake first thing in the morning, and then he'd go out and shoot a tiger!'

'Did *you* ever shoot a tiger?' I asked, accepting a glass from Mehmoud and adding a chunk of ice to the milkshake.

'I shot a leopard once,' said Mehmoud. 'I wasn't supposed to touch the guns, but one morning, after his milkshake, Carpet-sahib said I could accompany him into the jungle, provided I brought along a large thermos full of mango milkshake. It was a hot, humid morning and Carpet-sahib was soon feeling thirsty.

'"Hold my rifle, Mehmoud, while I have a drink," he said, and he handed me his gun and took the

thermos. While he was quenching his thirst, a *kakar*—a barking deer—appeared in the open, just fifteen to twenty feet in front of us. "Shall I shoot it, sir?" I asked. I'd seen him shooting many times, and I knew how the rifle worked. "Go ahead, old chap," he said. "Let's have some venison for dinner."

'So I put the rifle to my shoulder, took aim, and fired. It was the first time I'd fired a gun, and the butt sprang back and hit me in the shoulder, while the bullet itself whizzed over the deer and into the tree beneath which it was standing.

'Away went the *kakar*, while I held my shoulder in agony. I'd missed it by several feet. But then there was a terrible groan from the branches of the tree, and a huge leopard came crashing through the foliage, falling with a thud at our feet. It was quite dead, baba. 'I'd missed the *kakar* and shot a leopard. It must have been watching the deer, waiting to pounce on it, when it was struck by my bullet.

'"Good shot!" cried Carpet-sahib. "Well aimed, Mehmoud, I didn't see the leopard."

'"Nor did I, sir," I said.

'"But you shot it all the same," said Carpet-sahib.

'And since I did not want the skin, he rewarded me with five hundred rupees. The leopard was stuffed and kept in his verandah, to scare away the monkeys. Of course he told everyone what a good shot I was, although it was the last time he asked me to hold his gun.'

'Never mind,' I said, 'you shot the leopard, and you saved the life of the pretty deer. And your mango milkshake is the best in the world.'

'Thank you, baba,' said Mehmoud, refilling my glass. 'This is a good year for mangoes.'

And it was a good year for mango milkshakes. As I discovered.

.4.

WRESTLING A KING COBRA

Later that summer, I was sent to a boarding school in the hills, and it was several months before I saw Mehmoud again. In those days, boarding school food was awful—dull, tasteless, monotonous—and I missed Mehmoud's koftas and curries and cutlets. Variety is the spice of life. I missed his stories, too. But I regaled the other boys in the dormitory with Mehmoud's tales of man-eating tigers and other denizens of the jungle, and

everyone was envious of the fact that the great Jim Corbett's *khansama* was now my cook, and, in some ways, my personal storyteller, for not many had been privileged to hear his stories.

When the winter holidays came around, I was relieved to find that Mehmoud was still in our employ.

He celebrated my homecoming by making an extra-large Christmas cake. A plum cake, he called it, and it was full of good things like raisins, dates, cherries, figs, and, of course, plums.

The Christmas cake stood in the middle of our dining table, but it was in the kitchen that I conducted most of my conversation with Mehmoud.

'What was your most frightening experience?' I asked him. 'Your encounter with the tiger, or with the crocodile?'

'Oh, they were nothing compared to my fight with the king cobra.'

'A king cobra!' I gasped. 'That must have been really scary.'

'Truly it was, baba. We were spending Christmas in the jungle—Carpet-sahib, his sister, and some friend of theirs, and of course I was there with a couple of helpers to make sure that no one went hungry.

'Winters can be very cold in the Terai region, and at night we had to use blankets and *razais*. It was windy too, and we kept the tent flaps closed. I thought nothing could get into my tent, but I was wrong. I am a good sleeper, hard to wake—as your good parents well know—but in the middle of the night I woke up with a horrible sensation. Winding slowly across my face was the cold, scaly body of a large snake!

'And it wasn't only on my face that I felt the slimy creature. It was moving across my legs, up my right side and over my right upper arm. Was it one snake, or several, I wondered.

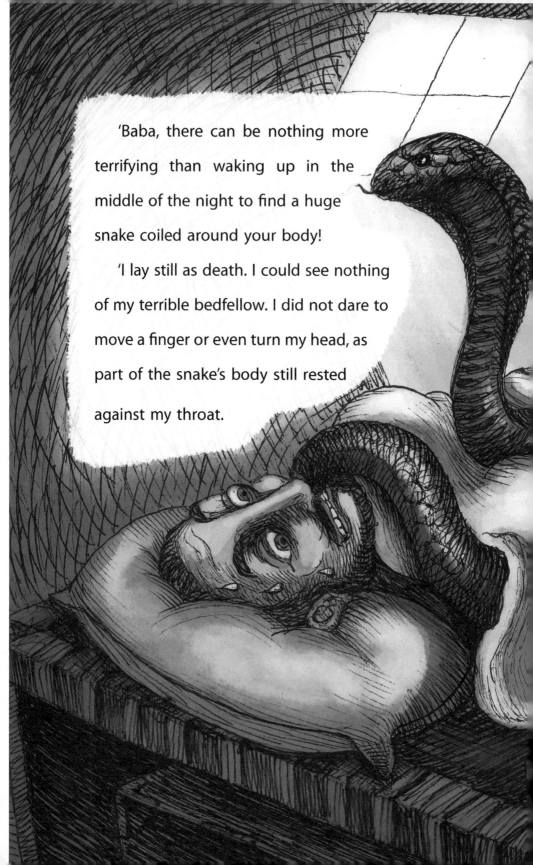

'Baba, there can be nothing more terrifying than waking up in the middle of the night to find a huge snake coiled around your body!

'I lay still as death. I could see nothing of my terrible bedfellow. I did not dare to move a finger or even turn my head, as part of the snake's body still rested against my throat.

'My mouth was parched and dry. So I sent a silent appeal to the Almighty, seeking his help.

'I think the snake was anxious to get out of my bed and out of the tent into which it had strayed, but had found itself trapped in the bedsheets and blanket. It passed on from my throat, moved down my waist, and crawled across my stomach. I could make out the snake's head—broad and blunt—only a few feet away from my face. Suddenly, it was still. Then it poked its black forked tongue in and out, while its body stiffened as it prepared to strike.

'I was covered in perspiration, and

I could hear my heart thudding. The snake must have heard it, too. Suddenly, it reared its head a foot in the air, and remained poised there, its cruel black eyes glistening in the moonlight. The slightest movement of hand or head, and those deadly fangs would be buried in my quivering flesh!

'I shut my eyes and waited in fear for the great snake to strike. But now it seemed to lose interest in my face, and once again it slithered down between my legs. A horrible sensation, baba! I was shivering all over. But then slowly I began to realize that the snake was not interested in me; it was interested only in getting out of my bed and out of the tent. I wanted to help it on its way. But if I made a sudden move, or leapt out of my bed, it would sink its fangs into me, of that I was certain.

'I remained still, trying to control my shivering. The snake was trying every corner of the bed, looking for an outlet. I felt its head against the palm of my hand. I could wait no longer. I grabbed the snake by its head, digging my finger into its under-jaw, and leapt to my feet, standing upright with that huge king cobra coiled around my waist. It writhed and tugged, trying its utmost to free its head and strike me dead. But I did not lose my hold on its head. I kept twisting its neck until it released its own hold on me and slithered out of the tent.

'That snake must have measured over seven feet in length, baba. Carpet-sahib could not believe I had fought it with my bare hands.'

'You have strong hands, Mehmoud,' I said, staring at his huge hands. I could well believe that he had wrestled a king cobra, and other creatures besides.

'Well, I need strong hands for chopping meat and making mutton cutlets for you, baba, not to speak of that Christmas cake, which was heavy going. Don't eat too much of it, baba, it's full of richness!'

But I failed to take Mehmoud's advice, ate too much cake, and spent most of Christmas Day in bed with a tummy-ache.

.5.

THE FACE BENEATH
THE PILLOW

'Camping in the jungle was full of danger,' I remarked. 'You must have felt much safer working in the house.'

'Well, cooking was certainly easier,' said Mehmoud. 'But I don't know if it was much safer. The animals couldn't get in, true, but there were ghosts and evil spirits lurking in some rooms. I changed my room, but there was always someone—*something*—after me. I don't know if I should tell you this, baba. You have your own small room and you may start imagining things…'

'I'm not afraid of ghosts, Mehmoud.'

'That's because you haven't seen one. Although, I'm not sure it was a ghost. And I did not actually see anything. But I felt it all right!'

'You can't *feel* a ghost, Mehmoud. At least, not in stories.'

Illustrations

'This wasn't a story. It was my first night in Carpet-sahib's house in the jungle. It was a big house with many rooms, and I was given one of my own. But there was no electricity in that out-of-the-way place. We used kerosene lamps or candles.

'I had brought my own *razai* and blanket, but the mattress was a strange one, and so was the pillow. It wasn't a pillow, really, but an old cushion, very hard and lumpy. It was my first night in that bed, and I was very uncomfortable. The candle burnt itself out, and I was still wide awake. I could see very little, there was just a small window allowing a little moonlight into the room. I was almost asleep when I heard someone groaning beside me. Groaning loudly, as though in pain. But there was no one else in the bed, and no one beneath it.

'The groaning stopped for a time, and then,

just as I was about to fall asleep, it started again.

Groan, groan, groan. Now it seemed

to come from beneath

my pillow.

'I turned on my side, and slowly, carefully, I slipped my hand beneath the pillow.

'It encountered a hairy face, a gaping mouth, hollow sockets instead of eyes. Horrible to touch! Not the face of a human, baba—the face of a *rakshas!*

'I tried to pull my hand away, but it was seized by that terrible mouth. A mouth with long, sharp teeth—teeth like daggers! It would have bitten my fingers off if I hadn't screamed and shouted for help.

'Carpet-sahib and his sister and the other servants came running. As they rushed into the room with torches and a lamp, those awful teeth released my hand.

'"Under the pillow!" I screamed. "Under the pillow!"

'They looked under the pillow. But there was nothing there. I showed them my fingers—they were bleeding badly.

'"A rat must have bitten you," said Carpet-sahib's sister. But she knew it wasn't a rat. And she gave me another room to sleep in.'

'And were you all right in the second room?'

'For a couple of nights, baba. Then it happened again.'

'You put your hand under the pillow again? And the face was there?'

'Not the whole face, baba. Just something soft and squishy.

'I thought it was a snail under my pillow. So I got up, lit my lamp, and looked under the pillow.'

'What was it, Mehmoud? Tell me quickly.'

'It was an *eyeball*, baba. An eye that had been removed from its socket. It was staring up at me. Just an eyeball—staring!

'I picked it up and threw it out of the window. I threw the pillow away, too. Something terrible had happened upon that pillow, I'm sure of it.'

'So it wasn't the room?'

'It wasn't the room. It was the pillow, baba. Next day, I went into town and bought a new pillow, and from then on I slept beautifully every night. Never use a strange cushion or pillow, baba. Terrible things have happened on pillows. So remember—when you return to school next month, take a new pillow, and don't use anyone else's!'

After listening to Mehmoud's story, I was always careful to use my own pillow. Even now, many many years later, I carry my own pillow wherever I go. No hotel pillows for me. You never know what might be lurking beneath them.

.6.

THE TIGER'S CLAW

'Why did you leave Jim Corbett and his sister?' I asked Mehmoud one day. 'Didn't they like your cooking?'

'I did not leave them, baba. They left me. That is, they left the country. Said goodbye to India. Went to live in Africa, where they hunted lions instead of

tigers. They gave me a certificate and some money, and I went home to my village near Shamli. There I sold guavas and mangoes. Very dull, after all that excitement with Carpet-sahib. Oh yes—and he gave me this.'

Mehmoud unbuttoned the top of his shirt and showed me a large tiger's claw in a locket that hung round his neck. 'It came from the last tiger that he shot before he went away. The claw of the last tiger.'

'Were you present when he shot it?'

'Yes, baba, I was there. It was the most exciting day of my life—if you don't count my wrestling match with the king cobra.'

'Did you wrestle with a tiger?'

'No, baba, I'm no match for a tiger. If I see a tiger, I run—I have strong legs. But on that particular day, I couldn't even run, I was alone in the bungalow and the tiger was coming for me.

'It was a man-eater all right, and I think it had come to take its revenge because of all the man-eaters that Carpet-sahib had shot. It was a big fellow, the largest tiger I have ever seen, and it walked right up to the verandah steps, raised its head and let out a terrific roar—it was like a challenge!'

'What did Corbett do?'

'He wasn't there. He and his sister had taken the jeep and driven into the town to see someone who wanted to buy the property. The rest of the staff were out, too. I was alone, setting the dining table for lunch,

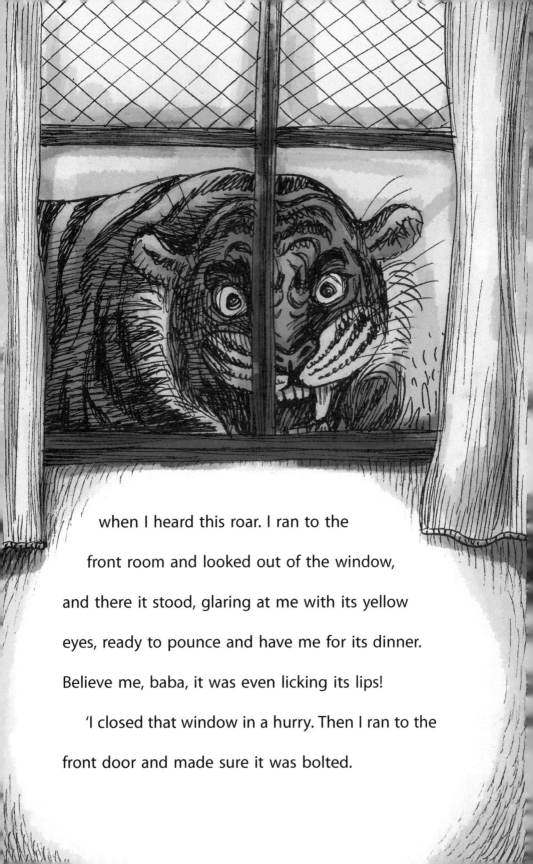

when I heard this roar. I ran to the

front room and looked out of the window,

and there it stood, glaring at me with its yellow

eyes, ready to pounce and have me for its dinner.

Believe me, baba, it was even licking its lips!

'I closed that window in a hurry. Then I ran to the

front door and made sure it was bolted.

'What next? I closed all the doors and windows—there were so many! Every time I looked out of a window I saw that tiger outside, circling round and round the house, just taking its time before leaping through an opening and pouncing on me—making a korma curry of me! It's nice cooking a keema or kofta curry, baba, but not so nice to be curry for a tiger!

'At last I had all the doors and windows shut. Let that tiger roar! I was safe from its claws. Or so I thought...

'I was standing in the middle of the front room, trembling with fear, when—thump, thump—its heavy paws began pounding on the front door.

'That door was strong—but not strong enough to stand against the strength and weight of an angry tiger. It would give way any minute. And then I would be mincemeat.

'There was a small skylight high up on the wall, which opened out on to the roof. If I could reach it and get through, I'd be safe on the roof.

'I pulled a table across to the wall and placed a chair on the table. I climbed on to it and reached the skylight. I squirmed through it and emerged on the roof. Then I looked down through the skylight just as the front door gave in, and the tiger rushed in, ready for dinner!

'But dinner was on the roof, out of its reach. That made it very angry. The tiger ran round the room, smashing chairs, upsetting the table. It charged into the other rooms, smashing and grunting, came back, angrier than ever, tore up a couple of rugs and bit

right through Carpet-sahib's tiffin carrier! And then, with an angry roar, it charged out of the house and into the garden.'

'But you were safe on the roof, Mehmoud!'

'So I thought. But when I stood up and moved to the edge of the roof, I saw the tiger looking up at me, judging the height from the ground to the rooftop. It was a distance of some twenty feet. Could a tiger leap that high? Even worse, there was an iron ladder leading from the open ground to the roof. The tiger had noticed this. It approached the ladder and began slowly, carefully, to climb up, rung by rung. In a few minutes, it would be upon me. What could I do?'

Mehmoud paused for effect, and all I could say was: 'Hide in the water tank?'

'There was no water tank. All I could do was send up a prayer to the Almighty.'

'And he must have heard you.'

'He did indeed, baba. And so did Carpet-sahib. For he returned just in time to see the tiger almost at the top of the ladder. He stood up in his jeep, raised his gun, and fired.

'Just one shot! Down came that tiger—

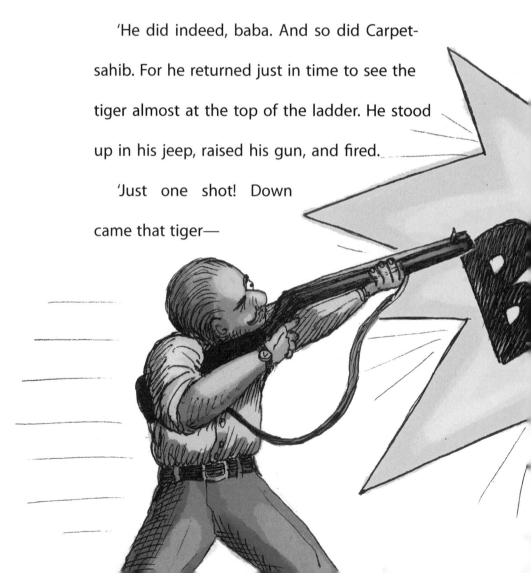

all in a heap—Carpet-sahib's last tiger.'

'It was yours, too,' I said. 'You were very brave. Jim Corbett must have been pleased with you.'

'Oh, *he* seemed pleased, but his sister was upset because of all the broken furniture and the smashed tiffin-carrier. I told her she would not need the stuff in Africa but she wasn't amused. Memsahibs are a bit funny and fussy about little things like furniture!'

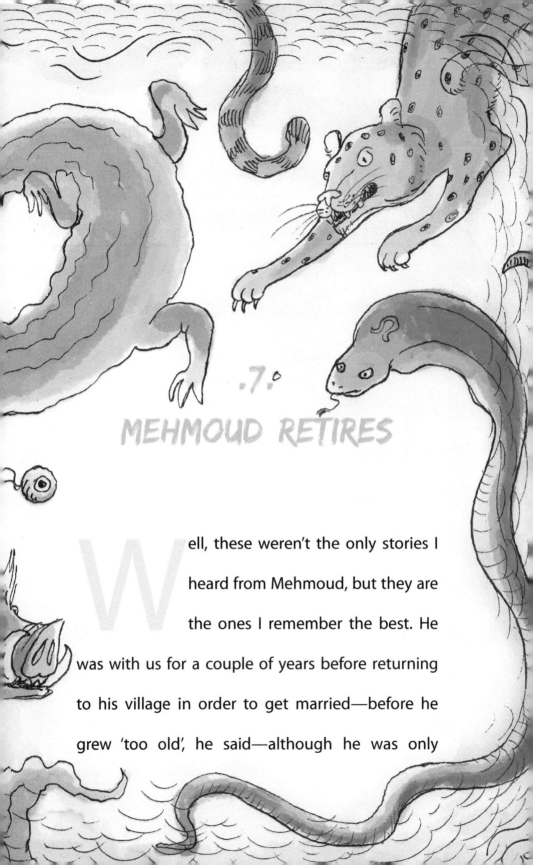

.7.
MEHMOUD RETIRES

ell, these weren't the only stories I heard from Mehmoud, but they are the ones I remember the best. He was with us for a couple of years before returning to his village in order to get married—before he grew 'too old', he said—although he was only

thirty. We heard later that he had settled down in his village, preferring the life of a cultivator to that of a cook. Working in our kitchen must have been pretty monotonous—no tigers ever came calling!

He was a wonderful cook, and I missed his cutlets and curries, his patties and pies, his sauces and stews, and his mango milkshakes. But most of all I missed his stories—even if they were a bit on the tall side!

MEHMOUD'S SAYINGS

To find adventure, follow a strange road
or try a new dish.

*

A life without surprises is a life with
no living.

*

What good is a full bank account
if your life is empty?

*

Flowers may fade,
but a true friend—never!

Lightning Source UK Ltd.
Milton Keynes UK
UKHW051517041019
350908UK00001BA/1/P